WEREWOLVES

THROUGHOUT
THE BRITISH ISLES

By

MONTAGUE SUMMERS

British Library Cataloguing-in-Publication Data
A catalogue record for this book is available
from the British Library

CONTENTS

MONTAGUE SUMMERS

Augustus Montague Summers was born in Bristol, England in 1880. He was raised as an evangelical Anglican in a wealthy family, and studied at Clifton College before reading theology at Trinity College, Oxford with the intention of becoming a Church of England priest. In 1905, he graduated with fourth-class honours, and went on to continue his religious training at the Lichfield Theological College. Summers entered his apprenticeship as a curate in the diocese of Bitton near Bristol, but rumours of an interest in Satanism and accusations of sexual misconduct with young boys led to him being cut off; a scandal which dogged him his whole life. Summers joined the growing ranks of English men of letters interested in medievalism and the occult. In 1909, he converted to Catholicism and shortly thereafter he began passing himself off as a Catholic priest, the legitimacy of which was disputed. Around this time, Summers adopted a curious attire which included a sweeping black cape and a silver-topped cane.

Summers eventually managed to make a living as a full-time writer. He was interested in the theatre of the seventeenth century, particularly that of the English Restoration, and was one of the founder members of The Phoenix, a society that performed neglected works of that era. In 1916, he was elected a fellow of the Royal Society of Literature. Summers also produced some important studies of Gothic fiction. However, his interest in the occult never waned, and in 1928, around the time he was acquainted with Aleister Crowley, he published the first English translation of Heinrich Kramer and James Sprenger's *Malleus Maleficarum* ('*The Hammer of Witches*'), a 15th century Latin text on the hunting of witches. Summers then turned to vampires, producing *The Vampire: His Kith and Kin* (1928) and

The Vampire in Europe (1929), and then to werewolves with *The Werewolf* (1933). Summers' work on the occult is known for his unusual, archaic writing style, his intimate style of narration, and his purported belief in the reality of the subjects he treats.

In his day, Summers was a renowned eccentric; *The Times* called him *"in every way a 'character'"* and *"a throwback to the Middle Ages."* He died at his home in Richmond, Surrey.

ENGLAND AND WALES, SCOTLAND AND IRELAND

IT is undoubtedly far more difficult for those living to-day to imagine the old England of peace and prosperity, than it is for those of us who remember our country before the dawning of the twentieth century to trace in our minds a similar picture. And even fifty years since, when we travelled at leisure and in security through some of the wilder parts of the kingdom, we could scarce believe that such a journey as we were taking under so pleasant and easy conditions was once an enterprise fraught with considerable danger owing to the numbers of ferocious animals that infested the very woods and glens and moors we were thus serenely traversing.

To-day the risks are no less than in ancient times, the British and Anglo-Saxon periods, although truly the perils are of a different kind. From one end of our island to another the roads are packed and ploughed by mechanical conveyances of the ugliest and most vicious pattern, swift engines of death and destruction, goaded to a maniac speed amid stench unutterable and the din of devils.

When we see London, despoiled of all her beauty, her nakedness uncovered, throwing out hideous suburban tentacles for mile after mile on all sides, it is impossible to realize that between the tenth and twelfth centuries there came up wellnigh to her gates, but a few fair meadows and open pasture lands intervening, vast forests in whose depths dwelt the stag, and the wild-boar and the bull.

Even at a comparatively modern period nearly the whole of the county of Stafford was either moor or woodland. Cannock

7

Chase alone measured no less an expanse than 36,000 acres. "The moorlands is the more northerly mountainous part of the county, lying betwixt Dove and Trent. . . . The woodlands are the more southerly, level part of the county, being from Draycote to Wichnor, Burton, etc. Between the aforesaid rivers, including Needwood-forest, with all its parks, are also the parks of Wichnor, Chartley, Horecross, Bagots, Loxley, Birchwood, and Paynesley (which anciently were all but as one wood, that gave it the name of woodlands)."[1] Maxwell forest, near Buxton, with the great forest of Macclesfield, the Peak forest, and the high Derbyshire moors united to make up "that mountainous and large featured district which in ancient times had been well timbered and formed part of the great midland forest of England".[2] From Nottingham to Manchester, and thence far on into Yorkshire, was one continuous forest, and there came to meet it the even wilder and larger forest of Bowland.

In Scotland all the district between Chillingham and Hamilton, some eighty miles, was completely wooded, and further north lay the huge Caledonian forest itself.

Inadequate and readily to be supplemented as are these few haphazard details, they will perhaps suffice to show what magnificent tracts of unreclaimed forest-land once existed here, affording through centuries an impenetrable fastness for wild beasts, and especially for the wolves whom year after year it seemed wellnigh impossible to exterminate and dislodge.

The forests of Reedsdale in Northumberland; Black-burnshire and Bowland in Lancashire; Richmond Forest comitatu Ebur; Sherwood Forest, Nottinghamshire; Savernake Forest in Wilts; the New Forest; the forests of Bere and Irwell; and many more are recorded as being the strongholds of packs of the most swift and savage wolves.

Of all British animals that have become extinct within historic memory the wolf was the last to disappear.[3]

Wolf-hunting was a favourite pursuit of the ancient Britons, and legend tells how wicked Mempricius (or Memprys), one of the descendants of old King Brute, a monarch who may have ruled Albion about 980 B.C., in that year fell a prey to the wolves whom he delighted to hunt with his great hounds, as old Andrew of Wyntoun[4] sings:—

> His brother he slew and syne all thai
> That he trowit wald thaim ma
> For to suceeid till him as king.
> It happinnit syne at a hunting
> With wolffis him weryit to be;
> Sa endit his iniquite.

Verstegan (Richard Rowlands), in his *Restitution of Decayed Intelligence in antiquities*,[5] writes of the Saxons: "The moneth which wee now call *Ianuary* they called *Wolf-monat*, to wit *Wolf-moneth*, because people are wont alwayes in that moneth to bee in more danger to bee deuowred of wolues, then in any season els of the yeare; for that through the extremitie of cold & snow, those rauenous creatures could not fynd of other beasts sufficient to feed vpon."

It is not without significance that in the *Poenitentiale*[6] of Egbert, Archbishop of York, who died 766, it is prescribed that "if a wolf shall attack cattle of any kind, and the animal so attacked shall thereof die, no Christian may eat of it". It would appear as though the wolf imparted by his very bite some demoniac quality to the beeves he had torn and slain.

Speaking of Flixton near Filey in Yorkshire, Camden[7] records that here "in King Athelstanes time was built an *Hospitall, for the defense* (thus word for word it is recorded) *of way-faring people passing that way from Wolues, least they should bee devoured.* Whereby it appeereth for certaine, that in those daies Wolues made foule worke in this tract, which now are no where to be seene in England, no not in the very marches toward Scotland; and yet within Scotland there be numbers of them in most places".

When Athelstan in 938 won so signal a victory at Brunanbrugh over Constantine, King of Wales, he imposed upon the defeated a yearly tribute of money, cattle, hawks, and keen-scented dogs, which mulct of gold and silver his successor, King Edgar, permitted Ludwall (or Idwal), the heir of Constantine, to exchange for the pelts of 800 wolves. It is generally stated that Edgar did this "to the intent the whole Countrie might once be clensed and clerely ridde" of these ravenous creatures, "whose carcases being brought into Lloegres, were buried at Wolfpit, in Cambridgeshire, and by that meanes thereof within the compasse and terme of foure yeres, none of those noysome creatures were left within Wales and England. Since this tyme also we read not that anye Wolfe hath beene seene here that hath bene bredde within the bondes and limites of our country."[8] The legend certainly grew and stuck fast that in this way the wolves were utterly exterminated, as poets loved to repeat. Thus Michael Drayton, in his *Polyolbion*,[9] 1612, the ninth song, has:—

Thrice famous *Saxon* King, on whom Time nere shall pray,
O *Edgar!* who compeldst our *Ludwall* hence to pay
Three hundred Wolues a yeere for trybute vnto thee:
And for that tribute payd, as famous may'st thou bee,
O conquer'd *British* King, by whom was first destroy'd
The multitude of Wolues, that long this Land annoy'd.

In his note Selden is careful to remark: "But this was not an vtter destruction of them; for, since that time, the Mannor of *Piddlesey* in *Leicester* shire was held by one *Henry* of *Augage*, per serjeantiam capiendi lupos, as the inquisition deliuers it."[10]

Edward Ravenscroft prefixed as a Preface to his tragicomedy *King Edgar and Alfreda*,[11] acted at the Theatre Royal late in 1677, "*The* Life *of* Edgar, *King of the* West Saxons," in which the tribute he imposed upon the Princes of Wales "To clear the Land from Wolves" is duly recorded, but there is no reference to this in the play as we should perhaps have expected, and it is rather surprising that there is no mention of wolves in Thomas Rymer's unacted "Heroick Tragedy", *Edgar, or The English Monarch*.[12]

William Somervile, in *The Chace* (1735),[13] has the following reference to "glorious Edgar":—

> Wise, potent, gracious Prince!
> His Subjects from their cruel Foes he sav'd,
> And from rapacious Savages their Flocks.
> *Cambria*'s proud Kings (tho' with Reluctance) paid
> Their tributary Wolves; Head after Head,
> In full Account, 'till the Woods yield no more,
> And all the rav'nous Race extinct is lost.

Even so serious and careful an author such as Dr. John Caius, in his *De Canibus Britannicis*, 1570,[14] when treating of the Sheep-Dog *Canis Pastoralis*, and taking occasion to mention the tribute paid to Edgar, quite confidently wrote that our shepherd's dog "hath not to deal with the bloud thyrsty wolf, sythence there be none in England, which happy and fortunate benefite is to be ascribed to the puisaunt Prince *Edgar* . . . Synce which time we reede that no Wolfe hath bene seene in England, bred within the bounds and borders of this countrey". He seems to have been little aware that the wolf had not become entirely extinct in England three-quarters of a century before, and did not entirely vanish from the British Isles until 200 years after his own day.

It is hardly necessary to review the ample evidence which shows the abundance of wolves in England during the period from the Norman Conquest until the beginning of the sixteenth century.

Guido, Bishop of Amiens, in his *Carmen de Bello Hastingensi*,[15] quite naturally relates that the Conqueror left the dead bodies of the English on the battle-field to rot and be devoured by beasts of prey:—

> uermibus, atque lupis, auibus canibusque uoranda,
> deserit Anglorum corpora strata solo.

The New Forest and the Forest of Bere, which, as we have noted, both teemed with wolves, were favourite hunting-grounds of the Red King and Henry I. It is chronicled in the *Annales Cambriae*[16] that in 1166 a mad wolf bit two and twenty persons, all of whom in a short space died.

In the reign of King John is said to have occurred the well-known circumstance of faithful Gellert being rashly slain by Prince Llewellyn, a story so familiar as it were superfluous to relate.[17]

Henry III not infrequently made grants of lands to various individuals upon the condition that these owners should hunt down and destroy the menacing wolves. Similar notices are found during the reigns of the three Edwards, Richard II, and the three Henries.

In his *Boke of Saint Albans*,[18] written about 1480 and printed at Saint Albans by the Schoolmaster-Printer in 1486, Dame Juliana Berners (or Barnes) includes the wolf among the "Bestys of venery":—

> Wheresoeuere ye fare by fryth or by fell
> My dere chylde take hede how Tristram dooth you tell
> How many maner beestys of venery ther were
> Lystyn to yowre dame and she shall yow lere
> Fowre maner beestys of venery there are
> The first of theym is the . hert . the secunde is the hare
> The boore is oon of tho . the Wolff and not oon moo.

There is hardly any hint afforded here that the wolf is becoming a particularly scarce animal, although relentless war had been waged against him from all sides for long enough. An old, but apparently unsupported, tradition says that the last wolf in England was killed at Wormhill Hall near Buxton in the county of Derby, and certainly it is probable that the royal Forest of the Peak, wild and of vast extent, would afford cover for the remnant of this savage tribe. Be that as it may, the reign of King Henry VII is certainly to be assigned as the term of the period to which the

12

wolf lingered here. Seventy years or so later George Turbervile in his *Booke of huntynge* writes: "The Wolfe is a beaste sufficiently knowen in Fraunce and other Countries where he is bred: but here in Englad they be not to be foud in any place. In Ireland (as I haue heard) there are great store of them."[19]

Long after he had been extirpated in England the wolf continued to be "rycht noysum to the tame bestiall in all partis of Scotland".[20] Camden at the end of the sixteenth century remarks that Strath-Navern, "the utmost and farthest coast of all Britaine," is "sore haunted and annoied by most cruell wolues", who not only set upon cattle but also "assaile men with great danger, and not in this tract onely, but in many other parts likewise of Scotland".[21] But a hundred years after Sir Robert Sibbald avers that the animal had been wholly exterminated. Although their numbers were no doubt greatly diminished, especially after the great hunts arranged in the days of James V (born 1512, died 1542) and Queen Mary, his daughter, actually it was not until the year 1743 that the last of the species was destroyed at a remote spot between Fi-Giuthas and Pall-à-chrocain.

One winter day the Laird of Macintosh was apprised that a large "black beast" supposed to be a wolf had been descried prowling in the glens, and less than twenty-four hours before had killed two children who were crossing the hills from Calder. A "Tainchel" or general drive was at once proclaimed, and amongst others summoned to the meet not the least important was a famous deer-stalker, MacQueen, who had the fleetest and strongest hounds in the country. All assembled at the tryst had waited long impatiently expecting MacQueen's arrival ere he appeared on the scene. Macintosh began to upbraid his unusual tardiness, when for answer the hunter lifted his plaid and threw the bleeding head of the wolf at the laird's feet, to be overwhelmed with congratulations and well feed in a generous gift of land for his prowess.[22]

Even later did the wolf maintain his hold upon Ireland, where formerly he existed in such numbers that a special breed of dog, a tall rough greyhound of exceptional size and power, and most highly esteemed, the Irish Wolf-hound, was especially reared to hunt the fierce and fearful packs. "They are not without wooloues and grayhoundes to hunt them, bigger of bone and limme then a colt," says Holinshed in his description of Ireland,[23] and Camden writes, "much noisance they have everywhere by Wolues." Thus in the *Travels of Cosmo the Third, Grand Duke of Tuscany, through England*[24] in 1669, wolves are spoken of as common in Ireland, which indeed had acquired and long kept the nickname of "Wolf-land".

"Wolves still abound too much in Ireland," Harting quotes from *The Present State of Great Britain and Ireland*, 1738; and in an article on the Irish Wolf-dog printed in *The Irish Penny Journal* for 1841,[25] Mr. H. D. Richardson says: "I am at present acquainted with an old gentleman between eighty and ninety years of age, whose mother remembered Wolves to have been killed in the county of Wexford about the years 1730–1740, and it is asserted by many persons of weight and veracity that a Wolf was killed in the Wicklow Mountains so recently as 1770."

In his *Origins of English History*[26] Charles Isaac Elton draws attention to the fact that there was no more usual periapt among the ancient Britons than "crescents made of the wolf's teeth and boars' tusks perforated and worn as charms". He also remarks, "We know that at one time the wolves swarmed in Sherwood and Arden"; and emphasizes that "the wolf and wild boar lingered until the end of the seventeenth century in the more remote recesses of the island", a generalization which is perhaps not strictly accurate, since, as we have seen, the wolf in England was extinct early in the sixteenth century, and in Scotland was not finally destroyed until the fourth decade of the eighteenth.

That werewolfism was a sorcery not unpractised by Anglo-Saxon warlocks is very certain, although the records are neither numerous nor detailed. It is not surprising that many erroneous beliefs had grown up concerning these demoniac wolves which the Bishops and priests were at some pains to correct.

In an old *Poenitentiale Ecclesiarum Germaniae*,[27] 151, occurs the following: "Hast thou believed what some were once wont to hold, namely that those who are commonly called *Parcae* can effect what they are often supposed to effect, namely that when a man is born they can direct and achieve his destiny, and moreover by a magic spell whensoever certain men will they are able to transform themselves into wolves, and such a one of this kind is called (*teutonica*) 'Werewulff',[28] or else they transform themselves into an other animal shape as they list. If thou hast believed that Man made in God's Image and Likeness can be essentially changed into another species or form by any power save that of Almighty God alone, thou must fast therefor ten days on bread and water."

In England a precisely similar clause, xv—"whosoever shall believe that a man or woman may be changed into the shape of a wolf or other beast . . ."—occurs in the *Poenitentiale*[29] (1161–2) of Bartholomew Iscanus, Bishop of Exeter, who died 1184. It should be carefully remarked that no denial of werewolfism is implied, that was far too real and too terrible a sorcery, but it is insisted that there must be a right theological understanding of this dark matter. For many had been reduced into giving the Devil an almost unlimited power, and thus betrayed into the most horrid impiety.

Although it has already been quoted, we may not impertinently remind ourselves of the well-known passage in Gervase of Tilbury's *Otia Imperialia*, written during the years 1210–14, where he speaks of the English werewolves, men who are thus metamorphosed at the changes of the moon,[30] adding that such shape-shifting was then by no means uncommon in this island. He returns to the same subject a little later in his work, and chapter cxx[31] is sufficiently important to be quoted in full: "*Of men, who were wolves.* It is often debated among the learned whether Nabuchodonosor during the allotted time of his penance was indeed essentially metamorphosed into an ox, since all theologians agree that 'twere easier to transform one shape into another than to create out of nothing. Some authors have written that he acted as an ox, and as a beast ate grass and hay, being an ox in all things his shape excepted. One thing I know that among us it is certain there are men who at certain waxings of the moon are transformed into wolves. In Auvergne—(the facts came under my personal observation)—a part of the diocese of Clermont, a certain great noble, Ponce de Castres, outlawed and exiled Raimbaud de Poinet, a valiant soldier, who had long carried arms. When thus banished and become a wanderer on the face of the earth, what time Raimbaud was wandering all alone, as if he had been some wild animal, making his weary way through trackless and untrodden paths, it happened that one night there fell upon him a damp and sore amaze, and he grew frantic being changed into a wolf, under which shape he marauded his own native village, so that the farmers and franklins in terror abandoned their cottages and manors, leaving them empty and tenantless. This fearsome wolf devoured children, and even older persons were attacked by the beast, which tore their flesh grievously with its keen and savage teeth. At last a certain carpenter was bold enough to attack the aggressor, and with a swift blow of his axe lopped off one of the beast's hind paws, whereupon the werewolf at once resumed human shape. Raimbaud publicly acknowledged that he was right glad thus to lose his foot, since such dismembering had rid him for ever of the accursed and damned form. For it is commonly reported and held by grave and worthy doctors that if a werewolf be shorn of one of his members he shall then surely recover his original body.

"In the neighbourhood of Chalus, in the diocese of Mende and the department of Ardèche, there lived a man, Calcevayra by name, who was a werewolf. Now he at the plenilune was wont to go apart to a distant spot and there stripping himself mother-naked he would lay all his clothes under some sheltered rock or thornbush. Next, nude as he was, he rolled to and fro in the sand until he rose up in the form of a wolf, raging with a wolf's fierce appetites. With gaping jaws and lolling tongue he rushed violently upon his prey, and he used to explain that wolves always run with open mouths because this helps them to sustain their fleetness of foot. If they close their mouths they cannot easily unclench their teeth, wherefore they are more likely to be captured if by any chance they are pursued."

It were to be wished that, deeply interesting as are the histories he relates, Gervase of Tilbury had given us examples of werewolfism—and he must have known plenty of such instances—from England rather than from the south of France. It should be remarked that there exists from very ancient times a certain connection between the wolf and outlawry, the ritual of this procedure being essentially religious in character, as was clear enough from the ceremonial employed. In the *Lex Salica* of the old Franks we have the phrase: "wargus sit," "propie est, *eiectus, exue*" as Dom Bouquet glosses.[32] An early Norman Law prescribes as the punishment of certain crimes "wargus esto", which is to say "Become a wolf", so that anyone may pursue and slay the criminal, cutting him down as if he were a wolf, a savage beast.[33] The Laws of S. Edward the Confessor (about 1050), "De Hiis qui Pacem Ecclesie fregerint," concerning fugitives from justice have: "Et si postea repertus fuerit et teneri possit, uiuus regi reddatur, uel caput ipsius si se defenderit; lupinum enim caput geret a die ut lagacionis sue, quod ab Anglis wluesheued nominatur. Et hec sententia communis est de omnibus ut lagis."[34] A statute of Henry I runs: "Et si quis corpus in terra, uel noffo, uel petra, sub pyramide uel structura qualibet positum, sceleratus infamacionibus effodere uel exspoliare presumpserit, wargus habeatur."[35] In *The Tale of Gamelyn*,[36] a spurious poem which Urry added to the list of Chaucer's works and Tyrwhitt removed, these lines occur in reference to Gamelyn being outlawed:—

Tho were his bonde-men . Sory and nothing glad,
When Gamelyn her lord . wolves-heed was cryed and maad.

A later instance of this word occurs in one of the Towneley plays, *The Buffeting*[37] (c. 1460), where raging Caiaphas cries:—

17

Now wols-hede and out-home on the be tane!

During the autumn of 1216 King John Lackland was ravaging the eastern counties of England. On 3rd October he sacrilegiously pillaged the church of good S. Guthlac at Croyland, after which, having lost all his baggage and many of his men in crossing the Welland, he pushed on in a black rage to the Cistercian abbey of Swineshead, near Bolton, where he surfeited himself by supping to excess on peaches and a kind of March ale. An attack of dysentery followed with fever. None the less he had himself conveyed to Newark, where he arrived on the sixteenth, by which time it became evident that the end was rapidly approaching. His physician, the Abbot of Croxton, shrived and houselled the dying king, who expired on the nineteenth of the month. As his will directed, he was buried in Worcester Cathedral, before the high altar.

At once strange legends began to fly abroad. In *The Brut, or The Chronicles of England*,[38] chapter clv, we already have the fully developed story of a monk at Swineshead, who appalled at the king's wickedness and the famine he swore to bring on England, went forth into the garden, where he found a toad which he pierced with a pin through and through till the venom had wholly infected a cup of lordly make. This he took and filled with humming ale, which he brought to John before whom he bent the knee lowlily, saying, "Sir, Wassail! for never days of your life drank you of such a cup." "Begin, monk," quoth the king. So the monk drank a draught, and the king drained the goblet after him. Then the monk incontinently repaired to the infirmary, and presently breathed his last. On whose soul God have mercy. Amen! And dirige with requiem shall be sung for him so long as the Abbey stands. But the bad king died within a few days, on the morrow after S. Luke.

Other chroniclers tell a different tale. Walter of Hemingburgh, the Austin Canon of Our Lady of Gisburn, writes how the lewd king, hearing that the Abbot of Swineshead had an exceedingly fair and virtuous sister, dispatched his pandars to bring her to him, being determined to enjoy her. Whereupon a monk of the house poisoned certain goodly pears of which the monarch ate, but not without first requiring the donor to eat of them also.[39]

The story that King John was poisoned by a monk of Swineshead has passed into the great body of Protestant tradition and even to-day is sometimes repeated. That half-crazed furious fanatic John Bale did not neglect to use it in his clouterly play *King Johan*,[40] the original draft of which was probably penned about 1538–1540 and considerably revised some two and twenty years later. Bale has the effrontery to hold up King John as a great and good monarch, a very father of his country. The legend of the poison furnishes a dramatic episode in *The Troublesome Raigne of King John*,[41] a foul and odious polemic, but the genius of Shakespeare utterly rejected the thing, even at the expense of losing what might well have been some powerful and not ineffective scenes.[42]

The story, however, which concerns us is that the evil monarch could not sleep in his tomb betwixt the shrines of S. Oswald and S. Wulstan,[43] those two blessed prelates, to the latter of whom in dying he had particularly recommended his soul.[44] Walter of Hemingburgh tells us, however, that he might not rest in his buriels.[45] Terrible noises, shrieks, howling, and other nocturnal disturbances were heard about the haunted grave,[46] until at last the Canons of Worcester disinterred his accursed body and flung the vile carcass, which had been embalmed by the Abbot of Croxton, out of the sanctuary on to a tract of unconsecrated ground, and he was verily Lackland whose rotting corse, the blackened features distorted in a hideous grin, had not even six foot of earth for a grave. But after death he became a werewolf,[47] and was seen abroad in this horrid shape, so that all men were greatly afraid. It is very curious that King John should become a werewolf after death, and one suspects there may be some confusion here, and that he became a vampire. For, as we know, in Germany, Serbia, and modern Greece it is believed that a

19

werewolf is doomed to be a vampire after death.

Actually very few accounts of werewolfism in England and Scotland have survived. Mr. Elliott O'Donnell[48] gives an instance of a werewolf haunting in Cumberland, where in a newly-built house far from any town a phantom "nude and grey, something like a man with the head of a wolf—a wolf with white pointed teeth and horrid, light eyes", was seen. There had previously been disturbances and howlings heard in the vicinity of the house. In a cave among the hills hard by were discovered a number of bones, among which was a wolfs skull and a human skeleton lacking the head. These were burned, and the hauntings ceased.

The same author mentions "the tall grey figure of a man with a wolf's head", a ghost seen in the Valley of the Doones, Exmoor. He records a similar phantom as having appeared in a lonely district of Merionethshire, and speaks of two particular spots in Wales, "one near Iremadac and the other on the Epynt Hills, where, local tradition still has it, werewolves once flourished."

There has been related to me the story of a werewolf incident[49] which occurred in the late eighties of the last century. An Oxford professor, being an ardent fisherman, had taken a small cottage for the summer on the shores of one of the remoter lakes in Merionethshire, among the hills, and here he and his wife were entertaining a guest. Whilst wading one day a few yards into the lake he stumbled over an object which seemed upon examination to be the skull of a dog belonging to an uncommonly large breed. Desirous of investigating further he carried it back to the house, where it was temporarily placed on a kitchen shelf. That evening his wife had been left alone awhile, and to her surprise not unmixed with fear she heard a snuffling and scratching at the kitchen door which led into the yard. Hesitant lest she should be confronted with a fierce dog, she went into the room to make sure the door was barred. As she moved something drew her attention to the window, and there she saw glaring at her through the diamond panes the head of a huge creature, half animal, half human. The cruel panting jaws were gaping wide and showed keen white teeth; the great furry paws clasped the sill like hands; the red eyes gleamed hideously; it was the gaze of a man, horribly intensive, horribly intelligent. Half-fainting with fear she ran through to the front door and shot the bolt. A moment after she heard heavy breathing outside and the latch rattled menacingly. The minutes that followed were full of acutest suspense, and now and again a low snarl would be heard at the door or window, and a sound as though the creature were endeavouring to force its entrance. At last the voices of her husband and his friend, come back from their ramble, sounded in the little garden; and as they knocked, finding the door fast, she was but able to open ere she fell in a swoon at their feet. When her senses returned, to find herself laid on the sofa and her husband anxiously bending over her, she told in halting accents what had happened. That night, having made all secure and extinguished the lamps, the two men sat up quietly, armed with stout sticks and a gun. The hours passed slowly, until when all was darkest and most lonely the soft thud of cushioned paws was heard on the gravel outside, and nails scratched at the kitchen window. To their horror in a stale phosphorescent light they saw the hideous mask of a wolf with the eyes of a man glaring through the glass, eyes that were red with hellish rage. Snatching the gun they rushed to the door, but it had seen their movement and was away in a moment. As they issued from the house a shadowy undefined shape slipped through the open gate, and in the stars they could just see a huge animal making towards the lake into which it disappeared silently, nor did a ruffle cross the surface of the water. Early the next morning the professor took the skull, and rowing a little way out from the shore flung it as far as possible into the deeper part of the tarn. The werewolf was never seen again.

Here we have a phantom werewolf whose power for evil and ability to materialize in some degree were seemingly energized by the recovery of the skull.

There is a story of a werewolf which was seen by certain shepherds on lonelier hill-sides at night about the middle of the eighteenth century, and there is a tale of a woman who was terribly scared one evening owing to the appearance of a great furry dog with the eyes of a man, which, so far as I can learn, must have been about a hundred years ago, but both of these grow faint with the passing of time. It would not be at all extraordinary if werewolfism survived in the lonelier districts of Wales even at the present day.

It is doubtful whether Holinshed is referring to a werewolf in his *Historie of Scotland*,[50] "Straunge Sightes seene," when he writes: "Also a sort of Woolues in the night season set upon suche as were keeping cattayle abroade in the fieldes and carried away one of them to the woodes, & in the morning suffred him to escape from amongst them againe." In any case he is speaking of a misty and legendary period.

Mr. Elliott O'Donnell gives two examples of werewolfism in Scotland of comparatively recent years. The one occurred in the Hebrides, and in its details resembles the Merionethshire incident I have just told. The other, which is in some sense more interesting, as relating to a live werewolf and not a phantom, concerns "a mon with evil leerie eyes and eyebrows that met in a point over his nose", named Saunderson, who dwelled in a cave of Ben MacDhui and who was a known werewolf. His forefathers, too, who had also inhabited the cave, were in their day more than suspect of lupine shape-shifting. As I read, Saunderson would have lived towards the end of the eighteenth century.

To come to an even later date, namely, some ten or at most fifteen years ago, a shepherd who was then occupying a lonely hut in a remoter tract of Inverness-shire, a man described to me as possessing unusually piercing eyes and heavy brows which met so as almost to form an arched bar across the forehead, was commonly reputed to be a werewolf, and certainly the evidence seemed conclusive on this point.

Such cases, however, are rare, and it is clear that even King James, a far more sceptical mind than is vulgarly supposed, had never investigated a case of lycanthropy at first hand, inasmuch as in his *Daemonologie*[51] (1597), the following passage occurs, the interlocutors being Philomathes and Epistemon: "*Phi.* And are not our war-woolfes one sorte of these spirits also, that hauntes and troubles some houses or dwelling-places?

"*Epi.* There hath indeede bene an old opinion of such like thinges; For by the *Greekes* they were called λυκανθρωποι, which signifieth men-woolfes. But to tell you simplie my opinion in this, if anie such thing hath bene, I take it to haue proceeded but of a naturall super-abundance of Melancholie, which as wee reade, that it hath made some thinke themselues Pitchers, and some horses, and some one kinde of beast or other. So suppose I that it hath so viciat the imagination and memorie of some, as *per lucida interualla*, it hath so highlie occupyed them, that they haue thought themselues verrie Woolfes indeede at these times; and so haue counterfeited their actiones in goeing on their handes and feete, preassing to deuoure women and barnes, fighting and snatching with all the towne dogges, and in vsing such like other bruitish actiones, and so to become beastes by a stronge apprehension, as *Nebuchad-netzar* was seuen yeares; but as to their hauing and hyding of their hard & schellie sloughes, I take that to be but eiked, by vncertaine report, the author of all lyes."

Nevertheless it was dangerous to accuse anyone of werewolfism. In the Records of the Presbytery of Kelso, 6th November, 1660, a memorial is noted that "Michell Usher, or Wishart, at Sproustoun, and Mausie Ker his wife, complean of John Broun, weaver ther, for calling him a warwoof, and her a witch".

There is no mention of the metamorphosis into a wolf in such authorities as George Sinclar, *Satans Invisible World Discovered*,[52] Edinburgh, 1685; *A History of the Witches of Renfrewshire*, Paisley, 1809; Dr. Samuel Hibbert-Ware, *A Description of the Shetland Islands*,[53] 1822; Charles Kirkpatrick Sharpe, *A Historical Account of the Belief in Witchcraft in Scotland*,[54] 1820 (1884); Sir Walter Scott, *Letters on Demonology and Witchcraft* (Murray's Family Library), 1830; Sir John Graham Dalyell, *The*

Darker Superstitions of Scotland,[55] 1834; the Rev. John Gregorson Campbell,[56] *Superstitions of the Highlands & Islands of Scotland*, Glasgow, 1900, and *Witchcraft & Second Sight in the Highlands & Islands of Scotland*, Glasgow, 1902; H. Drummond Gauld, F.S.A. Scot., *Ghost Tales and Legends*, 1929; Alexander Poison, F.S.A. Scot., *Our Highland Folklore Heritage*, Inverness, 1926, and *Scottish Witchcraft Lore*, Inverness, 1932.[57]

With regard to Wales also, neither William Howells, *Cambrian Superstitions*,[58] 1831; nor Wirt Sikes, *British Goblins*, 1880; nor even the Rev. Elias Owen in his exhaustive study, *Welsh Folk-Lore*,[59] 1896; nor Professor John Rhŷs, *Celtic Folklore, Welsh and Manx*,[60] 1901; has any mention of werwolfery.

On the other hand, most, if not indeed all, of these writers afford very detailed and considerable evidence concerning the shape-shifting of witches, especially to cats or hares.

Although strictly speaking this metamorphosis, which is generally accomplished by glamour, lies a little outside our province (however nearly akin to it), it cannot be entirely ignored in this connection. I am very well aware that it requires more chapters than I am able to afford pages for a consideration of so important a shape-shifting which should be in any sense deemed adequate or more than a mere touching upon it most lightly in passing.

Gervase of Tilbury writes[61]: "I know from mine own experience that certain women when prowling about at night in the form of cats have been espied by those who were quietly watching in silence and in secret. When these animals have been wounded, upon the very next day the women bear on their bodies in the numerical place the wounds inflicted upon the cat, and if so be a limb has been lopped off the animal, they have lost a corresponsive member." This author, accordingly, fully recognizes the phenomenon of repercussion.

In the *Malleus Maleficarum*,[62] part ii, question i, chapter 9, is related how a workman, living in a certain town of the diocese of Strasburg, was one day chopping wood when he was attacked by three great cats, biting and scratching him. He drove them off with great difficulty, bruising and beating them. To his surprise he was an hour later arrested, and brought before the judge. Nor could he for some days learn the charge since the judge was angry, supposing him to be obstinate in denying the truth. At length he was told he had on such a day at such an hour assaulted three ladies and batooned them so severely they were lying sick abed. Now he knew that was the very time he had driven off the cats, and he revealed the whole matter to the magistrates. Amazed at the event, yet convinced of the sincerity of the man, they realized it was the work of the Devil and dismissed him privily enjoining silence.

Sprenger and Kramer point out that this appearance of the three witches could have happened in two ways. Either the women were converted by glamour into the shape of cats; or else their three familiars in the likeness of cats attacked the man. In this latter case the blows received by the demons would be instantaneously transferred to the women. Our authors are of opinion that the first method is most likely.

This incident is recorded by several writers as worthy of remark. I find it, for example, in Bodin, *Démonomanie*, livre II, vi; and in Boguet, *Discours*, c. xlvii.

Bartolomeo Spina in his *Quaestio de Strigibus*[63] holds it as certain and proven that by the exercise of black magic and evil glamour witches can and do appear in the shape of cats.

LES LUPINS
By Maurice Sand

In the year 1566, during the witch-trials of the Evreux district, some terrible and extraordinary evidence was forthcoming. In an old and ancient castle at Vernon[64] a number of sorcerers were wont to assemble for their Sabbat. Four or five rash investigators resolved to watch the proceedings, only to find themselves assailed by a multitude of fierce cats. One of the company was killed by the bites and scratchings of these demoniacal animals, whilst the flesh of the others was shockingly ploughed and torn by their talons. None the less they succeeded in maiming and wounding some of the rout. The next day certain persons long suspect of witchcraft were found to be strangely injured and hurt.[65]

Boguet supplies many instances of this metamorphosis which came under his own experience.[66] One such adventure happened to a man named Charcot of the bailiwick of Gez. Another took place at the Château de Joux, when a traveller wounded a wild cat with his carbine. On arriving at the next inn he found the hostess had just been hurt in the hip by a shot from a carbine.

Paul Sébillot speaks of a sabbat of witches under the glamorous form of cats held in the haunted forest of Bonlieu, and also of two notorious sorceresses, la Dame de Florimont, who lived in the Rossberg (Hautes Vosges) district, and was eventually burned as a witch; and Madame de Badon, of the Château de Marçay, near Chinon, both of whom were adepts in the foul craft of shape-shifting.[67]

In 1875–6 the Rev. Wentworth Webster learned the following in the district of the Labourd: "Witches still appear in the shape of cats, but generally black ones. About two years ago we were told of a man who, at midnight, chopped off the ear of a black cat, who was thus bewitching his cattle, and lo! in the morning it was a woman's ear, with an earring in it. He deposited it in the Mairie, and we might see it there; but we did not go to look, as it was some distance off."[68]

In English trials for witchcraft the metamorphosis of the accused into a hare or a cat is often brought forward in evidence.[69] One example of each, which shall be chosen from later cases, may be adduced.

At the Summer Assizes held at Taunton before Justice Archer in 1663, Julian Cox, aged about seventy years, was indicted for practising witchcraft. The evidence upon which she was found guilty was overwhelming, but the point that concerns us here is "The first Witness was an Huntsman, who swore that he went out with a pack of Hounds to hunt a Hare, and not far off from *Julian Cox* her house, he at last started a Hare. The *Dogs* hunted her very close, and the third ring hunted her in view, till at last the Huntsman perceiving the Hare almost spent, and making towards a great Bush, he ran on the other side of the Bush to take her up, and preserve her from the Dogs. But as soon as he laid hands on her, it proved to be *Julian Cox*, who had her head groveling on the ground, and her globes (as he exprest it) upward. He knowing her, was affrighted, that his Hair on his Head stood on end; and yet spake to her, and askt her what brought her there. But she was so far out of Breath, that she could not make him any answer. His Dogs also came up with full cry to recover the game, and smelt at her, and so left off hunting any further. And the Huntsman with his Dogs went home presently, sadly affrighted".

This account is given by Joseph Glanvil in his *Saducismus Triumphatus*,[70] a work which even so complete an agnostic as W. E. H. Lecky[71] was compelled to acknowledge as—in his own phrase—"probably the ablest book ever published in defence of the superstition," a belief in the supernatural, whilst Glanvil himself, he candidly wrote as philosopher, scholar, and thinker, "has been surpassed in genius by few of his successors."

It does not seem possible that any reasoning and unprejudiced mind should cavil at the evidence of this witness in the trial. It is a plain, straightforward, and essentially veracious statement of fact. Yet, Glanvil remarks, some halfwitted people thought he swore false, which "*I suppose was because they imagined that what he told implied that* Julian Cox *was turned into an Hare. Which she was not, nor did his report imply any such real Metamorphosis of her body, but that these ludicrous Daemons exhibited to the sight of this Huntsman and his Doggs the shape of an Hare, one of them turning himself into such a form, and others hurrying on the body of* Julian *near the same place, and at the same swiftness, but interposing betwixt that Hare-like Spectre and her body, modifying the Air so that the scene there to the beholders sight, was as if nothing but Air were there, and a shew of Earth perpetually suited to that where the Hare passed. As I have heard of some Painters that have drawn the Sky in a huge large Landskip, so lively that the Birds have flown against it, thinking it free Air, and so have fallen down. And if Painters and Juglers by the tricks of Legerdemain can do such strange feats to the deceiving of the sight, it is no wonder that these Airy invisible Spirits as far surpass them in all such prœstigious doings as the Air surpasses the Earth for subtilty*".[72]

Glanvil's explanation is interesting and quite admissible. Indeed, it differs only in an unessential detail from the traditional and accepted explanation of glamour, which myself I might perhaps be rather disposed to prefer in this case of the witch Julian Cox.

There is an interesting allusion to the hare-metamorphosis of witches in Matthew Morgan's *Poem Upon the Late Victory over the French Fleet at Sea* (1692)[73]:—

So Huntsmen think they have a Hare in view,
And do with eager Cries her Flight pursue.
But when Sagacious *Jouler* comes so near,
To seize her hinder Legs and pluck to tear,
Comidia is Couchant in the Thorn,
And by their half-spent Mouths a Witch is Torn.

One of the latest—although perhaps quite strictly speaking not the very last—of witch-trials in England was the case of Jane Wenham,[74] the "Wise Woman of Walkerne", who on 4th March, 1711–12, was brought before Mr. Justice Powell at Hertford Assizes. Extraordinary interest had been roused, not only throughout the district but even in London, where the accused became "the discourse of the town". The evidence proved overwhelming, and in spite of the efforts of Justice Powell, whose attitude showed him to be entirely sceptical, Jane Wenham was formally condemned, only to be reprieved forthwith and soon pardoned.

There were many witnesses, and Anne Thorn, who had been bewitched by Jane Wenham, "saw Things like Cats appear to her" and "always before a Fit she saw a Cat, which would not only appear to her, but speak, and tell her several Things, tempting her to go out of Doors. It was also taken notice of that a dismal Noise of Cats was at that Time, and several Times after, heard about the House, sometimes their Cry resembling that of Young Children, at other Times they made a Hellish Noise, to which nothing can be resembled; this was accompany'd by Scratchings, heard by all that were in the House, under the Windows, and at the Doors, which startled and affrighted them all to a great degree; and several People, particularly *James Burvile, Thomas Ireland*, and others, saw these Cats, sometime Three or Four in a Company, which would run to *Jane Wenham*'s House whenever any Body came up to them." Anne Thorn also deposed that "*in the Morning of the 26th of* February, *as she was lying in bed, she saw a Cat sitting in the Window, which spoke to her*". Naturally in a great fear "*she hid her Head in the Bed-cloathes*", and presently the cat vanished.

Thomas Ireland was sworn, and deposed "That he hearing a Noise of Cats crying and screaming about the House several Times, went out, and saw several of them, which made towards *Jane Wenham*'s House; that he saw a Cat with a Face like *Jane Wenham*".

"*James Burvile* was also sworn, who said, That hearing the Scratchings and Noises of Cats, he went out, and saw several of them; that one of them had a Face like *Jane Wenham*."[75]

Various sceptical and agnostic pamphleteers with "plentiful Scatterings of *Billingsgate* Language" soon began to assert "The Impossibility of Witchcraft", but they were very ably and convincingly answered by Dr. Francis Bragge, who had impartially inquired into the case. As might be expected, Grub Street made a mighty jest of the apparition of a cat which spoke as something "very ridiculous and incredible", but Dr. Bragge fairly clinches the matter by his answer: "Is it more ridiculous and incredible, that an evil Spirit should assume the Shape of a Cat, and in such a Shape speak so as to be heard and understood, than that the Devil should speak to *Eve* in the Shape of a Serpent? Which we are oblig'd to believe upon the Credit of Divine Revelation."[76]

I myself have known in my own experience an instance of a witch who assumed the shape of a cat (Oxfordshire), and also a similar metamorphosis into a hare (Devonshire). In both cases I make no doubt there was glamour induced by the black art.

In *Memories of Hurstwood, Burnley, Lancashire*,[77] by Tattersall

Wilkinson and J. F. Tattersall, is given an interesting account of an old woman, by name Sally Walton, who lived at Cloughfoot Bridge in that district, some forty or fifty years before, and who was reputed a witch. A farmer, who dwelt near, awaking one night saw a large black cat sitting at his feet and watching him intently. Laying hold of a knife which was close at hand the farmer hurled it at the cat, striking one of its fore-legs. The animal vanished, leaving no trace anywhere. The very morning after it was noticed that old Sally had her corresponding arm wrapped in a kerchief, and there was not a neighbour but believed that she had assumed feline shape and visited the farmer's cottage, being wounded by him.

Some cat and hare incidents are recorded by the Rev. W. Henry Jones, of Mumby Vicarage, Alford, in *Lincolnshire Notes and Queries*,[78] October, 1889. A parishioner once told this gentleman that she saw a white rabbit in the churchyard, which being chased into the south porch vanished. At Hogsthorpe there was a hare no dogs could ever catch. One day, passing the house where a reputed witch lived, they heard a great noise, and entering found the old woman being chased about by dogs. The Rev. W. H. Jones' servant from Kirton Lindsey said: "One night my father and brother saw a cat in front of them. Father knew it was a witch and hammered it. Next day the witch had her face all tied up, and shortly afterwards died." "A story of a wizard taking the form of a hare and being slain was told to me a few miles west of Alford." At Grasby a witch who entered a house as a cat was attacked and beaten only to disappear. A little later a woman died, and those who laid out the body saw it was marked just in the same places where the cat had been struck.

Mr. W. Self Weeks, writing in the *Transactions of the Lancashire and Cheshire Antiquarian Society*, vol. xxxiv (1916),[79] relates that he was told by a farmer of Grindleton, near Clitheroe, that a weaver once found a cat near his loom which he in vain tried to drive away. At last in a rage he took a piece of rope and strangled the animal. The next day an old woman long held to be a witch was found dead in her bed. A farmer at Milton related that a few years ago a good house belonging to the Duke of Devonshire, near Bolton Abbey, fell vacant. There were many applicants, and it was eventually let to a man whose family were old tenants of His Grace. He took possession, but was not allowed a moment's peace. When he went to bed he was troubled by bad attacks of nightmare, which he seemed to hear enter his room in spectral form and wellnigh throttle him in a violent grasp. He consulted several doctors who were unable to afford relief, and at last he visited a well-known "wise man" at Leeds. The wise man told him that a certain woman, a neighbour, was at the bottom of the mischief. He was bidden lay a scythe by his bed ready to hand, and when the nightmare seemed to be upon him, to start up and slash at it through the air several times. He followed the instructions implicitly, and was never troubled again. The next morning, however, he heard that a woman who lived near had been taken suddenly and mysteriously ill. She was confined to her bed, and although she lingered many months before she died, she could never walk again. Her name was Hannah H——, an elderly woman, a regular chapel-goer, and esteemed a highly respectable person.

Mrs. Ella Mary Leather, in *The Folk-Lore of Herefordshire*,[80] writes: "Witches can change themselves into the form of animals, usually bats or black cats. A man from Eardisley, going one night to see a neighbour on the Kington Road, whose wife was a reputed witch, met a large black cat at the garden gate. Entering, he asked the man how his wife was. 'Didn't you meet her,' was the answer. 'She has only this minute gone out through the door there!' 'So it was certain after that,' my informant added, 'she was a witch, right enough.' . . . At Much Marie (near Ledbury) it was believed that witches became hares in order to lead the foxhounds off the right scent."

The famous Mrs. Anna Eliza Bray, in that most interesting work, *The Tamar and the Tavy*,[81] recounts the story of an old witch, living near Tavistock, who when she needed money would assume the shape of a hare and bid her grandson inform a certain ardent Nimrod who resided hard by that a hare was to be found in a given place. The lad was thus always sure to receive a good vail. At length, as the hare could never be caught, suspicion was aroused, and on one occasion when the old woman and her grandson were seen to leave their cottage the hounds were held in readiness to prevent them. The chase was speedier then than the witch cared, and she had only got within her cottage and resumed her shape when the huntsman accompanied by a justice and the parson of the parish were at the door which upon her refusal to open they forced. They found the old hag bleeding, covered with wounds, and still panting, hard breathed. She denied she had cozened them in the shape of a hare, but when they threatened to call in the pack she confessed her sorceries.

With regard to Scotland, I have collected a not inconsiderable amount of evidence, some from oral sources, but this must be reserved for a special study of the subject. At the present it will suffice to refer to the instances given by the Rev. J. G. Campbell in his *Witchcraft & Second Sight in the Highlands & Islands of Scotland*, to which study attention has already been drawn. He mentions the various forms in which the warlock may be disguised—ravens, rats, mice, black sheep, "and very frequently cats and hares." "The stories of witches assuming the shape of hares are numberless. . . . When a witch assumes this shape it is dangerous to fire at her without putting silver, a sixpence or a button of that metal, in the gun. If the hare fired at was, as indeed it often was, a witch in disguise, the gun burst, and the shot came back and killed the party firing, or some mischance followed. Old women used, therefore, to recommend that a sixpence be put in the gun when firing at a hare."[82]

A very remarkable account is given in Charles St. John's *Wild Sports and Natural History of the Highlands*[83] of the tranvection of a witch "possessed of more than mortal power After having long plagued the countryside with her sorceries she is said to have been brought down one night as she skirled through the air by a pot-valiant old soldier who loaded his gun with a double charge of powder and in place of shot a crooked sixpence and some silver buttons. Well-lined with whisky he fired when he saw her "just coming like a muckle bird right towards him". In the morning he was found lying half-asleep and half in a swoon, his gun burst beside him, and a fine large heron shot through and through on the ground, "which heron as everyone felt assured was the cailleach herself". The place where this happened is a bleak cold-looking piece of water known as Lochan-na-cailleaich (the witch's tarn), and Donald the beater who told the story added: "her ghaist is still to the fore, and the loch side is no canny after the gloaming." Allowing for natural exaggeration there is certainly a true story here.

W. N. Neil, in a study *Witch-Cats in Scotland*,[84] remarks: "The murderous ferocity of these Highland witch-cats compared to the milder nature of their sisters in the Lowlands almost leads one to think that it was not the common domestic cat that was the therianthropic shape chosen by the northern witches, but that of the spitting, swearing, untameable wild-cat which is a prominent representative of the Highland fauna to this day. The same conjecture may also explain the absence of the true werwolf from Scottish story, although the actual wolves persisted in its mountains and its moors till the eve of the Battle of Culloden. The wild-cat being comparatively common and noted for its cruelty and ferocity would be a far more suitable disguise for a witch than a sporadic and possibly timid wolf." The timidity of the wolf may be questioned.

The Rev. Elias Owen, in his *Welsh Folk-Lore*, to which reference has already been made, gives a large number of instances of witches transforming themselves into cats or hares. One example of each must briefly suffice. On the road between Cerrigydrudion and Bettws-y-Coed stood an inn kept by two women, sisters, of prepossessing manners and appearance, which, however, acquired an ill-name owing to the mysterious robberies that occurred in the house, although travellers confessed that the doors of their rooms always remained locked in the morning just as they had fastened them the night before. The parson of Llan Festiniog[85] resolved to unravel the business. Accordingly he obtained a lodging at the hostelry, but on going to bed kept a candle burning in the room. As he feigned sleep two cats stealthily crept through a narrow partition, and approaching his clothes seemed to fumble them with their paws as though feeling for his purse. Like lightning he struck with his sword and amid terrible screams the animals disappeared. Next morning only one of the sisters waited on him, and he was informed the other sister was indisposed. However, he forced his way to her presence and found that her right hand was bandaged just where he had wounded the cat. He then revealed who he was, and solemnly exhorted them to abandon their shape-shifting and sorceries.

The following incident happened to the Rector of Llanycil a few years before *Welsh Folk-Lore* was written, and is therefore an entirely modern example. When his servant was churning milk it was found that in spite of her efforts the milk would not churn. Upon removing the lid, however, out leaped a huge hare and ran off at full speed, whereupon the milk came easily enough. A wise man in Wales said that a witch in the shape of a hare could only be caught by a black greyhound. Mr. Owen also notes the unlucky omen of a hare crossing the path, and gives an interesting example.

C. I. Elton, in his *Origins of English History*,[86] writes that "The oldest Welsh laws contain several allusions to the magical character of the hare which was thought to change its sex every month or year, and to be the companion of witches who often assumed its shape". In Western Brittany hares are much feared. Essex Smith, in his *Fairies and Witches in Old Radnorshire*,[87] has several examples of hare and cat transformations. "Witches in the form of hares were numerous in Radnorshire. One huge hare, grey with extreme age, lived on Clyro Hill for many years; she could neither be shot nor caught with harriers or greyhounds; and was believed by all the countryside to be a witch. She had her regular rounds, and every morning early she came and sat under a bush near Tynessa."

The Manx witches are known as *butches*, which is probably nothing more than a variant of the English word. They are credited with the power of shape-shifting and their especial metamorphosis is that of the hare, when they are so fleet that only a black greyhound can catch them, and no shot save it be silver can hurt them. In Wales, generally speaking, only women can appear as hares, but in the Manx tradition both men and women assume this shape. This property is also said to run in certain families, and Professor Rhŷs in his *Celtic Folklore*[88] mentions a smith in the neighbourhood of Ramsey who was known as *gaaue mwaagh* "the hare smith". A witch if wounded as a hare resumes the human shape and the spell is broken, but the hurt always remains.

The cat-transformation is known in the Channel Islands, and here also werewolfery was once rife, but the tradition wanes. Sir Edgar MacCulloch in his *Guernsey Folk Lore*,[89] a book of the deepest interest, says: "The 'Varou', now almost entirely forgotten, seems to have belonged to the family of nocturnal goblins. He is allied to the 'Loup-Garou' of the French, and the 'Were-Wolf' of the English, if, indeed, he is not absolutely identical with them. He is believed to be endowed with a marvellous appetite, and it is still proverbially said of a great eater 'Il mange comme un varou'.

" 'Aller en varouverie' was an expression used in former times in speaking of those persons who met together in unfrequented places for the purposes of debauchery or other illicit practices. Thus one night such a one was heard saying that the time was propitious 'pour aller en varouverie sous l'épine'. *Varou* was originally from the Breton *Varw*—'the dead'—and was identified with the 'Heroes' or beatified warriors who were, by Homer and Hesiod, supposed to be in attendance on Saturn. Guernsey, in the days of Demetrius, was known by the name of the Isle of Heroes, or of Demons, and Saturn was said to be confined there in a 'golden rock' bound by 'golden chains'."

In Guernsey the word *varou* still lingers in place-names. The "Creux des Varous" is a subterranean cavern, which extends, folk say, from Houmet to L'Erée; a plot of ground near the cromlech of L'Erée ("Le Creux des Fées") is still known as "Le Camp du Varou", and an estate in the parish of S. Saviour is called "Le Mont-Varou". "Old people still remember that it used to be said in their youth that 'Le Char des Varous' was to be heard rolling over the cliffs and rocks on silver-tyred wheels, between Houmet and the Castle of Albecq, before the death of any of the great ones of the earth; and how this supernatural warning was sure to be followed almost immediately by violent storms and tempests."

"Sorcerers have the power of taking the forms of different animals, but when thus disguised cannot be wounded but by silver.

"A Mr. Le Marchant, 'des grent mesons,' had often fired at a white rabbit which frequented his warren, but without success. One day, however, beginning to suspect how the case really stood, he detached his silver sleeve-button from his wrist-band, loaded his gun with it, took a steady aim, and fired. The rabbit immediately disappeared behind the hedge. He ran up, and, hearing some person groaning as if in great pain on the other side, looked over and recognized a neighbour of his, a lady of the Vale, who was lying with her leg broken and bleeding profusely from a fresh wound."

The evidence for werewolfism in Ireland is of immemorial antiquity and persists through the centuries. Lycanthropy was believed for the most part to run in families, and an early tradition in the *Cóir Anmann* (*Fitness of Names*) has: "Laignech *Fáelad*, that is, he was the man that used to shift into *fáelad*, i.e. wolf-shapes. He and his offspring after him used to go, whenever they pleased, into the shapes of the wolves, and, after the custom of wolves, kill the herds. Wherefore he was called Laignech *Fáelad*, for he was the first of them (the group composed of Laignech and his descendants) to go into a wolf-shape." [90] This was in Ossory.[91]

From the *Leabhar Na H-Uidhri* (*The Book of the dun Cow*),[92] the oldest volume now known entirely in the Irish language, we learn that the Druids practised the magic art of shape-shifting.

An old Irish legend, which is given in *Kongs Skuggsjo (Speculum Regale)*, a Norse book compiled about 1250, runs as follows: "There is also in that land (Ireland) one wonderful thing, which will seem very untruthful to men. Yet the people who inhabit that land say that it is certainly true. And that befell on account of the wrath of a holy man. It is said that when the holy Patricius was preaching Christianity in that land, there was one great race more hostile to him than the other people that were in the land. And these men tried to do him many kinds of injury. And when he preached Christianity to them as to other men, and came to meet them when they were holding their assembly, then they took this counsel, to howl at him like wolves. But when he saw that his message would succeed little with these people, then he became very wroth, and prayed God that He might avenge it on them by some judgement, that their descendants might for ever remember their disobedience. And great punishment and fit and very wonderful has since befallen their descendants; for it is said that all men who come from that race are always wolves at a certain time, and run into the woods and take food like wolves; and they are worse in this that they have human reason, for all their cunning, and such desire and greed for men as for other creatures. And it is said that some become so every seventh year, and are men during the interval. And some have it so long that they have seven years at once, and are never so afterwards." [93]

I do not find this in the life of S. Patrick and the account of this Saint given by the Bollandists, under 17th March,[94] although one might have expected to meet with it in chapter xiii of the *Vita S. Patricii* by the Cistercian Jocelyn of Furness (*fl.* 1200), which has rubric *Patricio resistentes seuere castigantur.* Neither is the incident mentioned in the *Tripartite Life of S. Patrick*, but among the miracles of the Saint is recorded "Coroticus King of the Britons [changed] into the shape of a fox in his country".[95]

In the *Book of Ballymote*,[96] a miscellaneous collection

embracing historical, legendary, genealogical, and other matter, some of which is very ancient, compiled about the beginning of the fifteenth century, a passage says that "the children of the wolf" in Ossory could transform themselves and go abroad to devour people.

A Latin hexameter poem of the thirteenth century on the *Wonders of Ireland*, printed by Thomas Wright and J. O. Halliwell in their *Reliquiae Antiquae*,[97] has fourteen lines *De hominibus qui se uertunt in lupos*, which run: "There are certain men of the Celtic race who have a marvellous power which comes to them from their forbears. For by an evil craft they can at will change themselves into the shape of wolves with sharp tearing teeth, and often thus transformed will they fall upon poor defenceless sheep, but when folk armed with clubs and weapons run to attack them shouting lustily then do they flee and scour away apace. Now when they are minded to transform themselves they leave their own bodies, straitly charging their friends neither to move or touch them at all, however lightly, for if this be done never will they be able to return to their human shape again. If whilst they are wolves anyone hurts or wounds them, then upon their own bodies the exact wound or mark can plainly be seen. And with much amaze have they been espied in human form with great gobbets of raw bleeding flesh champed in their jaws." The same account, commencing "The descendants of the Wolf are in Ossory", is given in the Irish version (MS. D) of the *Historia Britonum* of Nennius of Bangor.[98]

Giraldus Cambrensis, in his *Topographia Hibernica*,[99] Distinctio ii, cap. 19, has the following account of werewolfery: "About three years before the arrival of Prince John in Ireland,[100] it chanced that a certain priest, who was journeying from Ulster towards Meath, was benighted in a wood that lies on the boundures of Meath. Whilst he, and the young lad his companion, were watching by a fire they had kindled under the leafy branches of a large tree, there came up to them a wolf who immediately addressed them in the following words: 'Do not alarm yourselves and do not be in any way afraid. You need not fear, I say, where there is no reason for fear.' The travellers none the less were thrown in a great damp and were astonied. But the wolf reverently called upon the Name of God. The priest then adjured him, straitly charging him by Almighty God and in the might of the Most Holy Trinity that he should do them no sort of harm, but rather tell them what sort of creature he was who spake with a human voice. The wolf replied with seemly speech, and said: 'In number we are two, to wit a man and a woman, natives of Ossory, and every seven years on account of the curse laid upon our folk by the blessed Abbot S. Natalis,[101] a brace of us are compelled to throw oft the human form and appear in the shape of wolves. At the end of seven years, if perchance these two survive they are able to return again to their homes, reassuming the bodies of men, and another two must needs take their place. Howbeit my wife, who labours with me under this sore visitation, lies not far from hence, grievously sick. Wherefore I beseech you of your good charity to comfort her with the aid of your priestly office.' When he had so said, the wolf led the way to a tree at no great distance, and the priest followed him trembling at the strangeness of the thing. In the hollow of the tree he beheld a wolfen,[102] and she was groaning piteously mingled with sad human sighs. Now when she saw the priest she thanked him very courteously and gave praise to God Who had vouchsafed her such consolation in her hour of utmost need.

"The priest then shrived her and gave her all the last rites of Holy Church so far as the houselling. Most earnestly did she entreat him that she might receive her God, and that he would administer to her the crown of all, the Body of the Lord.

"The priest, however, declared that he was not provided with the holy viaticum, when the man-wolf, who had withdrawn apart for a while, came forward and pointed to the wallet, containing a mass-book and some consecrated Hosts which, according to the use of his country, the good priest was carrying suspended from his neck under his clothing. The man-wolf entreated him not to deny them any longer the Gift of God, which it was not to be questioned, Divine Providence had sent to them. Moreover to remove all doubt, using his claw as a hand, he drew off the pelt from the head of the wolfen and folded it back even as far down as the navel, whereupon there was plainly to be seen the body of an old woman. Upon this the priest, since she so instantly besought him, urged though it may be more by fear than by reasoning, hesitated no longer but gave her Holy Communion, which she received most devoutly from his hands. Immediately after this the man-wolf rolled back the skin again, fitting it to its former place.

"These holy rites having been duly rather than regularly performed, the man-wolf joined their company by the fire they had kindled under the tree and showed himself a human being not a four-footed beast. In the early morning, at cock-light he led them safely out of the wood, and when he left them to pursue their journey he pointed out to them the best and shortest road, giving them directions for a long way. In taking leave also, he thanked the priest most gratefully and in good set phrase for the surpassing kindness he had shown, promising moreover that if it were God's will he should return home (and already two parts of the period during which he was under the malediction had passed) he would take occasion to give further proofs of his gratitude.

"As they were parting the priest inquired of the man-wolf whether the enemy (the English invader) who had now landed on their shores would continue long to possess the land. The wolf replied: 'On account of the sins of our nation and their enormous wickedness the anger of God, falling upon an evil generation, hath delivered them into the hands of their enemies. Therefore so long as this foreign people shall walk in the way of the Lord and keep His commandments, they shall be safe and not to be subdued; but if—and easy is the downward path to iniquity and nature prone to evil—it come to pass that through dwelling among us they turn to our whoredoms, then assuredly will they provoke the wrath of the Lord upon themselves also.'

"It so happened that about two years later when I was passing through Meath, the Bishop of that diocese had summoned a synod, and had requested the honourable attendance of the Bishops of neighbouring sees and my Lords the Abbots, in order that they might take counsel together concerning this incident which the priest had related to him. The Bishop, learning that I was travelling in those parts, sent two of his priests to me, asking me if it were possible to attend the synod at which a matter of such grave importance was to be deliberated, and, if indeed I could not assist in person, he begged me at least to give them my opinion and judgement in writing. When I had heard the whole circumstance in detail from the two priests (although indeed I had been told of it before by many others), inasmuch as I was prevented by many weighty affairs from attending the synod, I was fain amend for my absence by giving my advice in a letter. The Bishop and the full synod so far approved of my counsel, that they followed it forthwith, commanding the priest to travel to Rome, and there to lay the whole thing before the Holy Father,[103] delivering to him letters containing the priest's own account, which was certified by the seals of all the Bishops and Abbots who had been present at the conclave.

"It is not to be disputed, but must be most certainly believed that for our salvation the Divine Nature assumed human nature. Now in the present case we find that at God's bidding in order to manifest His supreme power and righteousness by a very miracle human nature assumed the form of a wolf.

"The point arises: Was this creature man or beast ? A rational animal is far above the level of a brute beast. Are we to class in the species man a four-footed animal, whose face is bent to the earth, and who cannot indulge in the visible faculty ? Would he who slew this animal be a murderer ? We reply that the miracles of God are not to be made the subjects of argument and human disputation, but are to be wondered at in all humility."

Giraldus, having come to this very admirable and sane

conclusion, then discusses the famous passages in S. Augustine, *De Ciuitate Dei*, xvi, 8, and xviii, 17 and 18.

He sums up: "In our own day also we have seen persons, who deeply skilled in magic arts, turned any substance which was of sufficient quantity into fat porkers as they seemed (but curiously they were always of a reddish hue), and these they sold in the markets. None the less the glamour vanished as soon as they crossed any water and the substance returned to its true material form. However carefully they were kept, they could not retain their spurious appearance more than three days.

"It is commonly known, and has been bitterly complained of in former days as well as now, that certain foul hags in Wales, as well as in Ireland and Scotland, change themselves into the shape of hares, and under this counterfeit form sucking the teats of cows they secretly rob other persons of their milk.

"We hold then with S. Augustine that neither demons nor sorcerers can either create or essentially change their natures; but those, whom God has created are able by His permission to metamorphize themselves so far as mere outward appearance is concerned, so that they appear to be what truly they are not, and the senses of men beholding them are fascinated and deceived by glamour, so that things are not seen as they really exist, but by some phantom power or magic spell the human vision is deluded and mocked inasmuch as it rests upon unreal and fictitious forms."

Camden,[104] writing of Wolf-men in Tipperary, says: "Whereas some of the Irish and such as would be thought worthy of credit, doe affirme, that certaine men in this tract are yeerely turned into Wolves; surely I suppose it be a meere fable: unlesse happly through that malicious humour of predominant unkind Melancholie, they be possessed with the malady that the Phisitians call Λυκανθρωπία, which raiseth and engendreth such like phantasies, as that they imagine themselves to be transformed into Wolves. Neither dare I otherwise affirme of these metamorphised *Lycaones* in *Liveland*, concerning whom many writers deliver many and meruailous reports."

Sir William Temple, in his essay *Of Poetry*,[105] commenting upon "those Trophies of Enchantment . . . Productions of the *Gothick Wit* . . . all the visionary Tribe of *Fairies, Elves,* and *Goblins,* of *Sprites* and *Bulbeggars*", continues: "How much of this Kind, and of this Credulity remained even to our own Age, may be observed by any Man that reflects so far as thirty or forty Years; how often avouched, and how generally credited, were the Stories of *Fairies, Sprites, Witchcrafts,* and *Enchantments?* In some Parts of *France,* and not longer ago, the common People believed certainly there were *Lougaroos,* or Men turned into Wolves; and I remember several *Irish* of the same Mind."

FOOTNOTES:

[1] A note by Sir Simon Degge, who was born in 1612 and lived to the age of 92. This note is printed in the Rev. Thomas Harwood's edition (1820) of Sampson Eredeswick's *Survey of Staffordshire*, pp. 2 and 3.

[2] Robertson, *Buxton and the Peak*, p. 41, quoted by Harting.

[3] The authoritative study is *British Animals Extinct within Historic Times*, by James Edmund Harting, F.L.S., F.Z.S., London, Trübner, 1880, an admirable work from which I have not hesitated to draw freely for details of the wolf in Great Britain and Ireland. Harting emphasizes (p. 204) that "in order to confine the subject within reasonable limits" he carefully abstains from any mention of the werewolf or wolf-legends. If I give any quotation from Harting, and not from the original source, I have been careful to mention this in the corresponsive note.

[4] *The Original Chronicle of Andrew of Wyntoun*, ed. F. J. Amours, The Scottish Text Society, vol. ii, p. 312 (Wemyss MS.), eh. xxxix, 11. 617–622.

[5] Antwerp, 1605, p. 59.

[6] Migne, *Patres Latini*, lxxxix, column 426, D. The *Poenitentiale* is now generally considered to be a Frankish compilation of the ninth century and largely drawn from Halitgar. See H. J. Schmitz, *Die Bussbücher und die Bussdisciplin der Kirche*, Mainz, 1883, Theil iii, Kapitel 4, "Poenitentiale Egberti," pp. 565–587.

7 *Britannia, Britain* . . . "Written first in Latine by *William Camden*, Clarenceux K. of A. Translated newly into English by *Philemon Holland* . . . Finally revised . . . by the said Author." Folio, Londini, 1610, Yorke-shire, p. 715.

[8] Raphael Holinshed, *The Firste volume of the Chronicles of England, Scotlande, and Irelande*, 1577; The Thirde Booke, cap. 7, "Of sauuage beastes and vermines," p. 108. Holinshed claims that England is "void of noysome beasts, as Lions, Beares, Tygers, Wolfes, and such like: by meanes whereof our countrymen may trauaile in safetie". Which cannot be said to-day.

[9] Folio, 1612, p. 135.

[10] Ibid., p. 144. Selden quotes as his authority: *Itin. Leicest. 27. Hen. 3. in Archiu. Turr*, Londin.

[11] 4to, 1677. Term Catalogues, Hilary, 28th February, 1678.

[12] 4to, 1678. Term Catalogues, Michaelmas, 26th November, 1677.

[13] 4to, 1735. Book the Third, 11. 13–19; pp. 50–1.

[14] Joannis Caii Britanni *de Canibus Britannis*. Liber Unus. Londini, per Gulielmum Seresium. 8vo, 1570. I have used the edition in *The Works of John Caius, M.D.*, ed. John Venn and E. S. Roberts, Cambridge, 1912, p. 10 (*De Canibus*), and quote the English version *Of Englishe Dogges*, by Abraham Fleming, 1576, as there reprinted, pp. 21 and 22 of the *Treatise*. Thomas Pennant, *Tours in Wales*, 1778–1781 (new edition, by Professor Rhys, 3 vols., 1883), remarks that "the report of *Edgar*'s having extirpated the race of wolves out of the principality, is erroneous," vol. i (1883), p. 113.

[15] *Monumenta Historica Britannica*, vol. i, pp. 856–872, *De Bello Hastingensi Carmen*, 11. 571–2; p. 867. Guy was Bishop of Amiens 1059 to 1075.

[16] Harl. MSS., No. 3859, ed. Williams, Rolls Series, pp. 50–1. "Apud

Kermerden lupus rabiosus duo de uiginti homines momordit qui omnes fere protinus perierunt." The MS. is believed to be a translation from the original Welsh.

[17] It is said that the story of Gellert is found in many literatures. It certainly resembles the tale of the Knight and his Greyhound in *The Seven Wise Masters*. See further, Heinrich Adelbert von Keller, *Li romans des sept sages*, Tübingen, 1830, p. clxxviii. William Robert Spencer's poem, *Beth-Gêlert, or The Grave of the Greyhound*, signed Dôlymelynllyn, 11th August, 1800, was privately printed (4 pp.) by Collingwood, Oxford, but not published. *Beth-Gêlert* was first published in *Poems* (pp. 78–86) by William Robert Spencer, London, Cadell and Davies, 1811.

[18] I have used the facsimile edition with introduction by William Blades, London, Elliot Stock, 1881. The allusion to Tristram is to Sir Tristram of the Table Round, who was a mighty hunter and a great authority on all matters of venery. He was popularly supposed to have been the author of many (if not all) hunting terms, and his name was constantly invoked to clench a statement, as it were.

[19] *The Noble Arte of Venerie or Hunting*, 4to, 1575, chapters 75 and 76. The pages are wrongly numbered, 363 and 362; followed by p. 205 to p. 214. Turbervile gives two chapters to hunting the wolf.

[20] *Heir beginnis the hystory and croniklis of Scotland*. John Bellenden's translation of Boece. Edinburgh, 1541. Ca. xi, "of the gret plente of haris, hartis, and vthir wild bestiall in Scotland." Sig. C. ii.

[21] Trans. Philemon Holland, ut cit. sup., *Scotia, Scotland*, p. 54.

[22] There are, of course, various stories concerning the killing of the last wolf who infested a certain district in Scotland, as for example the last wolf killed at Lochaber by Sir Ewen Cameron in 1680, which Pennant misunderstood to be the last wolf killed in Scotland: *British Zoology*, vol. i, p. 88, and *Tour in Scotland*, vol. i, p. 206. Surtees, *History and Antiquities of the County of Durham*, vol. ii, p. 172, gives 1682 as the date of the killing of the last wolf in Scotland. Sir Thomas Dick Lauder in his *Account*

of the Moray Floods of August, 1829, relates how MacQueen of Pall-à-chrocain slew the last wolf, but says that the scene of this exploit was in the parish of Moy, county Inverness. He also has another story of two old wolves and their cubs being killed at Knoch of Braemory, near the source of the Burn of Newton.

[23] Holinshed, op. cit., p. 9; Camden, op. cit., *Ireland*, p. 63. Cf. from MS. Rawl. B. 512: "As Paradise is without beasts, without a snake, without a lion, without a dragon, without a scorpion, without a mouse, without a frog, so is Ireland in the same manner without any harmful animal, save only the wolf, as sages say." *Tripartite Life of S. Patrick*, ed. W. Stokes, Rolls Series, part i (1887), p. xxx.

[24] "Translated from the Italian Manuscript in the Laurentian Library at Florence," London, 1821, p. 103.

[25] p. 354. This article was afterwards incorporated by the author in his *The Dog: its Origin, Natural History, and Varieties*, 1848. My reference to *The Irish Penny Journal* is from Harting, p. 202. In *A Brief Character of Ireland*, 12mo, 1692 (Licensed 16th Nov., 1691), a stupid enough squib, the peasants of remoter districts are described as "like their Native Wolves", p. 47.

[26] London, 1882: p. 149, p. 223, and p. 3.

[27] Herm. Jos. Schmitz, *Die Bussbücher und das Kanonische Bussverfahren*, ii Band, "Die Bussbücher und die Bussdisciplin der Kirche," Düsseldorf, 1898, p. 442.

[28] Variants are: weruvolff, Werewolf, werwolf, Werewl., and wertvoos.

[29] "Liber poenitentialis . . . per magistrum Bartholomaeum Exoniensem episcopum collectus . . ." British Museum, Cotton MSS., Faust. A. viii; 1.

[30] See Chapter I, n. 18.

[31] *Otia Imperialia*, ed. Felix Liebrecht, Hanover, 1856, pp. 51–2.

[32] Titulus, LVIII, i. *Recueil des Historiens des Gaules et de la France*, Paris, 1741, ed. Dom Martin Bouquet, O.S.B. (Maurist). Tom. iv, p. 154.

[33] Frédéric Pluquet, *Contes Populaires*, Rouen, 1834, 2me édition,

"Le Loup-garou," p. 15.

[34] Benjamin Thorpe, *Ancient Laws and Institutes of England*, 1840, vol. i, p. 445.

[35] Ibid., p. 591. Henrici Primi, lxxxiii, 5. The Laws of Henry I are now generally regarded as a twelfth-century compilation with a generic title.

[36] To be dated c. 1400. *Gamelyn*, 700–1. Chaucer, ed. W. W. Skeat, Oxford, 1894; vol. iv, *Canterbury Tales*, text. Appendix to Group A, p. 662. John Urry died 1715, and his edition of Chaucer was published posthumously in 1721. Tyrwhitt's *Canterbury Tales* was issued 4 vols., 1775; a fifth volume followed in 1778.

[37] No. xxi, ed. England and Pollard, *Early English Text Society*, 1897, p. 232, 1. 139. See also Lydgate, *Bochas*, vii, 1261.

[38] Ed. F. W. D. Brie, *E. E. Text Soc.*, 1906, part i, pp. 169–170.

[39] Walter of Hemingburgh, *Chronicon*, ed. H. C. Hamilton, London, 1848; vol. i, pp. 252–4.

[40] *The Dramatic Writings of John Bale*, edited by J. S. Farmer. Early English Dramatists, 1907. *King Johan* has been edited separately by J. H. P. Pafford, 1931.

[41] In two parts, 4to, 1591.

[42] It is, of course, true that in *King John*, Act V, scene 6, Hubert cries:—

The King I fear is poyson'd by a Monke, . . .

A Monke I tell you, a resolued villaine

Whose Bowels sodainly burst out:

and in the following scene the "fell poison" is spoken of, whilst the King himself exclaims: "Poyson'd, ill fare." But previous to all this on the battle-field, v, 3, King John had groaned:—

Aye me, this tyrant Feauer burnes mee vp, . . .

Weaknesse possesseth me, and I am faint.

The Troublesome Raigne of King John is gutter Protestantism, and as such of no account. Bowden in his *Religion of Shakespeare* (p. 120) acutely observes: "Shakespeare, in adapting it, had only to leave untouched its virulent bigotry and its ribald stories of friars and nuns to secure its popularity, yet as a fact he carefully excludes the anti-catholic passages and allusions, and acts throughout as a rigid censor on behalf of the Church." J. P. Chesney, *Shakespeare as a Physician*, 1884, comments on the cry "Poyson'd, ill fare" that "the case of King John bears a much closer analogy to a case wherein the hand of nature has been instrumental in saturating the system with poison, than it does to one in which a 'villainous Monk' had been the instrument. Miasmatic exhalations had no doubt wrought the evil in this case".

[43] "Coram altari magno in medio inter sacrosancta corpora Oswaldi et Vulfstani, pontificum beatorum." Nicolas Trivet O.P., *Annales*, ed. T. Hog, London, 1845, p. 197.

[44] Roger of Wendover, iii, 385.

[45] "Sepultus, dico, est, sed non cum honore regio, quia terra quae in operibus suis pessimis turbata extitit nondum ad plenum pacificata quieuit." Ed. cit., p. 254. Walter of Hemingburgh has a story of King John appearing "in uestibus quasi deauratis" and all fulgent with light to a certain priest, but he obviously doubts the tale, and indeed the vision may have been a diabolic illusion, although, as we hope, he was saved by the intercession of S. Wulstan.

[46] See Gabriel de Moulin, Curé de Maneual, *Histoire générale de Normandie*, livre XIV, xxxiii, Rouen, folio, 1631, p. 559.

[47] Amélie Bosquet, *La Normandie romanesque et merveilleuse*, Paris, 1845, chap, xii, p. 238.

[48] *Werwolves*, London, 1912, chapter vi, pp. 92–109.

[49] This is, I think, the same incident as was told by Mr. J. Wentworth Day in *The Passing Show*, 9th July, 1932, "Exploring the Uncanny—No. 4. The Terror on the Mountain," pp. 24-5. Mr. Day also mentions the werewolf seen by the shepherds, and the incident of the woman scared by the great dog with the eyes of a man.

[50] Ed. cit., pp. 40-1.

[51] Third Booke, chap. i, edited by G. B. Harrison, "The Bodley Head Quartos," 1924, pp. 61-2.

[52] I have used the reprint by Thomas George Stevenson, Edinburgh, 1871.

[53] "Witchcraft of Shetland," pp. 572–584, and notes, pp. 592–601.

[54] For which see Bibliography.

[55] It should perhaps be mentioned that the same author's *Rare and Remarkable Animals of Scotland*, 2 vols., London, 1848, deals with animal products resembling flowers, or shrubs, or trees, and "with other foliaceous products" (vol. ii, chapter i, p. 1) and various zoophytes, but does not treat of any quadrupeds.

[56] The Rev. John Gregorson Campbell was minister of Tiree 1861–1891, and the collections in his two books are especially valuable in that they were "Collected entirely from Oral Sources". In his *Witchcraft and Second Sight*, pp. 30–44, he deals with witches as sheep, hares, cats, rats, gulls, cormorants, whales.

[57] The Scotch and Welsh folklore contained in Κρυπτάδια, "Recueil de documents pour servir à l'étude des Traditions populaires," vol. ii, Heilbronn, 1884, although valuable, is almost entirely of an erotic nature and has no mention of werewolfery. This is also the case with the French, Polish, and Russian collections given in vol. v (Paris, 1898) of the same series.

[58] William Howells, the son of the Rev. J. Howells, vicar of Tipton, was only eighteen at the time he wrote this book.

[59] *Welsh Folk-Lore*, by the Rev. Elias Owen, M.A., F.S.A., of Llanyblodwel. Oswestry and Wrexham, 1906, pp. 224–233.

[60] 2 vols., Oxford, 1901; vol. i, pp. 293–6.

[61] *Otia Imperialia*, Tertia Decisio, xciii, ed. cit., p. 45.

[62] Eng. tr., ut cit. sup., pp. 126–7.

[63] 4to, Romae, 1576, cap. xix: "Experientiae apparentis conuersionis strigum in catos."

[64] Vernon on the Eure is some 25 kilometres from Evreux. The castle is of the thirteenth century. See Th. Michel, *Histoire de la ville et du canton de Vernon*, 1851; and E. Mayer, *Histoire de la ville de Vernon*, 2 vols., 1875–7.

[65] Bodin, *Demonomanie*, Liv. ii, ch. vi. See a note by M. F. Bourquelot, *Recherches sur la Lycanthropie: Mémoires de la Soc.*

des Antiquaires de France, tome xix (N. Série, torn, ix), Paris, 1849, pp. 246–7. Also Paul Sébillot, *Le Folk-Lore de France*, tom. iv, Paris, 1907, p. 195.

[66] *Discours des Sorciers*, 1590, ch. xlvii. Eng. tr. *Examen of Witches*, 1929, p. 142.

[67] Sébillot, op. cit., tom. i, p. 281, and tom. iv, pp. 304–5.

[68] *Basque Legends*, second ed., 1879, p. 70 n. The first edition is 1877.

[69] The shape-shifting of a witch is, of course, an entirely different thing from the appearance of a familiar in animal guise. None the less, Mr. G. L. Kittredge has persistently confused the two, and in consequence his chapter "Metamorphosis" (*Witchcraft in Old and New England*, 1928, pp. 174–184) presents an entanglement not a little difficult to unravel.

[70] London, 1681, the Second Part, Relation viii, pp. 190–1.

[71] *History of the Rise and Influence of the Spirit of Rationalism in Europe*, 2 vols., 1865; vol. i, p. 126, and p. 120.

[72] Ed. cit., Relation viii, p. 200.

[73] 4to, 1692, p. 18. For *Comidia* we should surely read *Canidia*.

[74] See Montague Summers, *The Geography of Witchcraft*, 1927, ch. ii, pp. 158–160.

[75] *A Full and Impartial Account of the Discovery of Sorcery and Witchcraft Practis'd by Jane Wenham of Walkerne in Hertfordshire . . . Also Her Tryal . . .* London, 1712, pp. 17, 23, 29.

[76] *Witchcraft Farther Display'd*, London, 1712, p. 38. Introduction signed F[rancis] B[ragge], Ardely-Bury, April the 3d, 1712. He remarks that even "while she is in Prison" the "wicked old Witch" Mother Wenham, "has found out a Way to get plenty of Money."

[77] 1889, pp. 57–8.

[78] Vol. i, part 8, pp. 244–9.

[79] Manchester, 1917, pp. 104–6.

[80] Hereford, 1912; "Witchcraft," p. 52.

[81] *A Description of the Part of Devonshire bordering on the Tamar and the Tavy*, 3 vols., London, 1836, vol. ii, pp. 277–9. For parallels to this story see Rev. Elias Owen, *Welsh Folk-Lore*,

1896, pp. 230–3, and Mrs. Ella Mary Leather, *The Folk-Lore of Herefordshire*, 1912, p. 52.

[82] Op. cit., pp. 6–8.

[83] Edited by the Rt. Hon. Sir Herbert Maxwell, Bt., London and Edinburgh, 1919, pp. 37–9. Charles St. John died in July, 1856.

[84] *The Occult Review*, August, 1924; vol. xl, No. 2, pp. 102–8.

[85] Huw Lloyd, 1533–1620, who was apparently regarded as possessed of extraordinary powers of exorcism. Parson Richard Dodge, who was vicar of Talland in Cornwall from 1713 until his death, aged 93, in January, 1746, enjoyed the same reputation. See Thomas Bond, *Historical Sketches of the Boroughs of East and West Looe*, 1823, pp. 154–5: "About a century since the Rev. Richard Dodge . . . had the reputation of being deeply skilled in the black art, and could raise ghosts, or send them into the Red Sea, at the nod of his head."

[86] London, 1882, p. 297.

[87] *The Occult Review*, June, 1921; vol. xxxiii, No. 6, pp. 352–9.

[88] Vol. i, p. 294.

[89] Edited by Edith F. Carey, London and Guernsey, 1903, pp. 230–2. For a witch as a white rabbit, pp. 360–1; sorcerers as hares, pp. 361–5. See also pp. 315–337, witchcraft trials.

[90] *Irische Texte*, ed. Whitley Stokes and Ernst Windisch, iii serie, 2 heft. Leipzig, 1897, p. 377 (No. 215).

[91] *The Irish Version of the Historia Britonum of Nennius*, ed. with a translation by James Henthorn Todd. Irish Archaeological Society, 1848, pp. 204–5, and note.

[92] A collection of pieces in prose and verse compiled and transcribed about 1100 by Moelmuiri Mac Ceileachair. A facsimile of the MS. (sixty-seven large quarto pages) was published Dublin, 1870. See 546 and 36 sqq.

For the heathenism of these transformations see *Irische Texte*, Stokes and Windisch, iii serie, 1 heft, Leipzig, 1881. [Do chuphur in da muccado]: suithi n-genntlecta la cectar-de in da mucuith 7 nus delbdais in cech riet . . . the learning of gentilism which enabled them to shift into any shape (p. 235).

The Rev. Edward Davies, *Mythology and Rites of the British Druids*, 1809, does not mention this art of shape-shifting. Mr. Lewis Spence, *The Mysteries of Britain*, 1928, also has no remark upon metamorphosis, but he refers to Sir J. G. Frazer's *The Golden Bough* (*Balder the Beautiful*, vol. ii, 1923, pp. 41–3—Mr. Lewis does not give the exact reference, which is this), where it is suggested that the men and animals burned to death at certain Celtic festivals were warlocks, and sorcerers disguised in brute form. This is, to say the least, extremely hypothetical, and in view of the evidence from the *Leabhar Na H-Uidhri* inadmissible.

[93] *Folk-Lore*, vol. v, No. 4, pp. 310–11. Kuno Meyer, The Irish Mirabilia.

[94] *Acta Sanctorum*, Martii tom. ii, Antwerpiae, 1668, pp. 517–592.

[95] *Tripartite Life*, ed. Whitley Stokes, Rolls Series, 1887; part i, p. 249 and note; part ii, p. 271 and note.

[96] Ed. Robert Atkinson, Dublin, 1887, 140*b*: "The Conarian Race of Ireland and Scotland."

[97] London, 1843, vol. ii, pp. 103–7. The poem is from MS. Cotton. Titus, D. xxiv, fol. 74, vo.

[98] Ed. Todd, 1848, ut cit. sup., pp. 204–5.

[99] Ed. by the Rev. James F. Dimock, *Works*, vol. v, 1867, pp. 101–7, Rolls Series. The book of Giraldus appeared in 1188, and was dedicated to Henry II.

[100] The adventure with the wolf-man took place in 1182 or 1183.

[101] S. Natalis, Abbot, is honoured as the founder of monasticism in North Ireland. The son of Aengus, he was of the royal family of Munster, and lived in the sixth century. He is the Patron of Invernaile, Donegal, and Kinnawly. Feast 27th January.

[102] "A female werewolf (*ben tét i cuanricht*) was called *conel*." *Irische Texte*, Stokes and Windisch, iii serie, 2 heft. Leipzig, 1897, p. 421.

[103] Lucius III (Ubaldo Allucingoli), elected to the Chair of Peter, 1st September, 1181; died at Verona, 25th November, 1185.

[104] Camden, op. cit., *Ireland*, p. 83.

[105] Temple, *Works*, 2 vols., folio, London, 1720. Volume the First,

part ii, *Miscellanea*, p. 244. There is an interesting allusion
to werewolfery in Giles Rose's *The Theatre of the World: or, A
Prospect of Humane Misery*, 1679, being a translation of Pierre
Boaistuau's *de Théâtre du Monde*, Paris, 8vo, 1558 (and many
subsequent editions). The passage (pp. 204–5) runs: "Others have
fancied themselves to be transformed into a Wolf, and ceased not
from running at Nights with the Wolves over the Mountains and
desart places, following their howlings and gestures through all
places in the Country, so greatly were they tormented with their
Distempers, till the Sun had cast her Beams and Rayes upon the
Earth: The *French* call this Distemper the *Loupos Garoux*; but
the Greeks call this sort of Sickness *Lycanthropeia:* A thing that
need not seem strange, nor fabulous to any that has read the holy
Scriptures, and in it the pitiful estate of *Nebuchadnezzar*, who
was transformed into an Oxe, for the space of seven Years, to
reduce him to the knowledge of his God, *Dan.* 4."